THE LAST STRAW

TALES OF WOMEN SCORNED

THE LAST STRAW

TALES OF WOMEN SCORNED

ISBN: 978-0-9834137-4-5

CAUSEY PUBLISHING COMPANY, ©Phyllis M. Causey 2014
EMAIL: phylliscausey@hotmail.com

Table of Contents

DREAMING

As a young child dreaming,

Seems I knew you then.

Oh, such marvelous dreams

A young mind can conceive.

I dreamed of you then.

I dream of you now.

But, I'm afraid to believe

In fairy tales and dreams

I'm afraid I'll awaken

And find you are gone.

"What time will you be here? Alright, I'll see you soon." Julie hung up the phone and headed for the bathroom.

"Who's coming over here?" Julie's eleven-year-old son, Danny asked. "What's his name?" He was following her.

"Where did you meet him?" Julie's fifteen-year-old daughter, Laurie demanded to know. "How long have you known him?" She was following Danny.

"Listen, you guys. His name is Robert. He's coming over for a while. I met him about a month ago. He likes me and I like him. We're not getting married or engaged and he's not moving in. He's just coming by to visit. Okay?" She checked her face in the bathroom mirror.

"Is he cute?" Laurie inquired. Julie applied some lipstick.

"Is he *cute*!" Danny mocked Laurie. "That's all you think about. Is he SMART! That's more important!"

"Ha! You wouldn't know smart if it bit you, Dummy!"

"Hey, hey! Calm down, you guys. And when Robert gets here, I want you two to be nice. Understand?" She ran the comb through her hair.

"What if we don't like Robert?" Danny put special emphasis on the name.

"Well..."

"Do we still have to be nice?" Laurie finished.

"Of course! Aren't I nice to your friends?" She laid down the comb and headed for the bedroom.

"Yeah, but you like my friends." Danny pointed out. He followed his mother. His sister followed him.

"How do you know that?" Julie examined herself in the full-length mirror. She turned as she studied all angles.

"Which one don't you like?" Danny persisted.

Julie stopped and faced him. "The point is that I allow you to choose your own friends and I trust you to make good choices. As long as they act nice, I assume that they ARE nice. Even if I am not fond of them, I don't interfere without very good reason."

"So, it doesn't matter what we think of him?" Laurie was cross-examining.

"Of course, it matters, but I keep in mind that you're both a little prejudiced!" She kissed Laurie. Then she grabbed Danny's face and kissed him, too.

"Ugh! You got lipstick on." He wiped his mouth with the back of his hand and looked at it very distastefully. "Ugh!"

The doorbell rang.

"Laurie, get the door for me, please."

"Sure, Mother." She left the room. Danny followed her.

Laurie opened the door. Robert stood there outside the door as these two little people stood staring at him.

"Hi. I'm Robert. Julie is expecting me." No response. "Uh... do you think I could come in?"

"MOM!" They shouted almost in unison and they kept their eyes on him. "He's here."

"Move, Dummy!" The girl pushed the boy out of the way and opened the door wider. "Come in. I'm Laurie, and this is my brother, Danny. We're Julie's kids. My mother will be in in a sec." Laurie left the room.

Robert sat down on the sofa. Danny sat down, too ... in the chair that faced the sofa. Robert couldn't believe he was so nervous. He wished this kid would stop staring at him.

"Hi." Julie came into the room.

Whew, Robert thought. He stood up as Julie approached him. He kissed her on the cheek very carefully as they were clearly under observation.

"You look marvelous, Darling!" He gave her the bouquet of flowers he had almost forgotten he was holding. "These are for you. They are not nearly as beautiful as you are."

"Why, thank you, Robert. They are beautiful. Did you pick them yourself?"

"Yes. As a matter of fact, I did."

"You have very good taste."

"I know." He looked at her to convey the deeper meaning of his words. He was making her blush.

They felt the eyes on them and looked together first at Danny and then the other way, at Laurie.

"You met my children, Laurie and Danny."

"Yes, I did."

"Uh... come with me, Robert. I'll find a vase for these. She started for the kitchen. The kids followed them. She stopped. Robert stopped. Laurie and

Danny almost collided into him and each other. "You guys can go watch TV.

"The movie isn't on yet." Said Danny.

"Well, just let me know when it is. Okay?

Laurie grabbed Danny's hand and yanked him. "Come on, Dummy. I told you, you wouldn't know smart if it bit you."

"Who you calling Dummy?" They disappeared into the back of the house. Julie and Robert laughed.

Great kids! Good company, huh? He asked.

"Sometimes..."

"Well, I got the once-over pretty good. I wonder what the popular consensus will be."

"I'm sure it will be interesting. They're pretty selfish when it comes to me, you know."

"Well, I guess I can understand that – not wanting to share you." His smile was captivating.

It had been a long time since Julie had met anybody she liked enough to bring home. Robert was the first man Julie REALLY liked after dating him for more than a month. He was handsome, sexy, intelligent, and attentive. He called her every day since they met. So far, she had resisted his urges toward sexual involvement, but she wanted him just as much. She just wanted to be sure, (if that is possible) that he was not seeking a one-night stand, a rebound affair, or just something to keep him busy since his "roommate" moved out about three months ago.

Robert said "it's time. Our relationship was really over a long time ago. I just didn't want to put her out, you know."

How fortunate for her, Julie thought. The rumors of a man shortage caused a lot of men to adopt the theory which made them feel like they could dominate women and have a few. Some women were so desperate, they were willing to share. They were happy to have anything that resembled a man. Julie had decided she would wait for a "good one." She wanted Mr. Right.

"Hey," Robert walked up to her. She had been so deep in thought. "You still with me?" He put his arm around her and pulled her close to him. "You smell so good."

Julie thought "He's so fantastic."

"Ma!" Danny yelled from the den. "The movie is coming on now."

"I guess we got our orders." Robert mumbled as he brushed her cheek with his lips. He pressed against her. His body was firm and hard. "Can we go to my place later?"

"You had better cut that out!" Julie kissed him on the mouth and pressed herself against him. Then she pushed him gently. "Let's go."

"How do you expect a man to keep his cool like that?" Robert mumbled as they headed for the den.

In the den, the seating arrangements were carefully thought out by Danny and Laurie. They occupied both ends of the sofa, which only left the chair and the middle seat on the sofa. Julie could see this was going to be an experience.
"Robert and I want to sit on the sofa, okay?"
"Why? He can sit on the chair and you can sit over here with us like you always do."

Julie tried to maintain her composure. "Because he is my guest and we want to sit together. So, move it!"

Danny and Laurie both jumped up. They looked at each other with the 'see-now-she-got-a-man-over' look. Laurie sat in the chair, while Danny seated himself on the floor in front of the TV, facing them. Julie looked at Robert, hunched her shoulders, smiled and said, "I told you. They're my kids."

Robert made a face like he was scared. He looked at Danny, who was watching him intently, and smiled. Danny, refusing to be persuaded, turned to look at the movie. "What movie are we watching, Danny?"

"Better Off Dead." Danny answered reluctantly and looked at Robert as if that title could be symbolic or something.

"O...kay." Robert decided he wouldn't press his luck. He put his arm on the back of the sofa. He was careful not to give the kids the wrong impression. He really wanted them to stop staring. "You have a beautiful home here." He whispered to Julie.

"Thank you." She reached for his hand.

Robert thought, "Danny won't like this." He tried not to look at Danny. He tried to concentrate on the movie.

"Some popcorn would be great right now." Said Julie.

"I'll pop some." Laurie offered. "I already saw this movie twice."

"That would be so nice of you, Laurie." Julie was proud of her daughter's generosity. It was as if her home training was showing through after all.

"Want to help me, Danny?"

Danny looked at her, looked at them, and said flatly, "No." He stared at the TV. Laurie left.

Robert played with Julie's hand. "Your hands are pretty. They are so dainty." Julie blushed. They stared at each other.

Danny came over to the sofa and took Julie's other hand. "Didn't you have six fingers on your hand?"

Julie looked at Danny. "Yes."

"What happened to the extra finger?" Danny queried.

"They cut it off when I was a baby. Danny, you know that."

Danny took the hand Robert had been holding. "Did you have one on this hand, too?" He turned it to expose the little bump that remained. "This is where it was, right?" Julie glared into Danny's eyes.

"Danny, you go help Laurie bring the popcorn. Bring the sodas too. Robert, would you like a soda?"

"Yes, thank you."

Danny looked at her.

Danny..." Julie's voice was threatening.

"I know, I know. You serve me and my friends. So, I gotta do the same for you and your friends, right?"

"It's nice of you to offer." Julie said through her teeth. Danny got up and left the room.

"That popcorn sure smells good, doesn't it?" Robert was laughing. He was glad Danny wasn't staring at him anymore.

Laurie came in carrying a big bowl. She set it on the cocktail table in front of her mother and Robert. "I'll be right back with the drinks."

Danny came in carrying two glasses. "Just bring ours, Laurie." He set one in front of his mother, and the other in front of Robert. Robert and Julie exchanged looks.

"Thank you, Danny." They said almost in unison.

Robert dug into the popcorn. "This popcorn is delicious."

"Thank you." Laurie said as she came in with the drinks for Danny and herself.

"Ma!" Danny was suddenly excited. "Watch this! This part is really funny."

The guy in the movie nearly broke his neck trying to ski down a mountain. It was obvious that this was probably his first time trying it. Everybody laughed.

"Hey! That is a beautiful portrait of you, Julie. Who drew it?" Robert pointed at a drawing of Julie that was hung on the wall.

"It's my favorite. I like it better than any picture I have of myself. I had it done at a festival. That guy was really good!"

"Yeah," Danny looked at the picture and back at his mother, "but one of your eyes is bigger than the other one." He moved closer to Julie for a closer look. "One of them really is, isn't it?"

Julie wanted to punch his little face in. Maybe she should take him to his room and let him have it! That would serve his butt just right!

"Danny!" She pushed him. "Go over there and watch your movie." She didn't want Robert to think these things really bothered her. She would KILL Danny later. She promised.

"Everybody is like that." Robert spoke up. "Didn't you know that? One foot is bigger, one hand... look at yours."

Danny inspected his hands. "Nope. I don't think so."

"Sure it is." Robert insisted. "You just can't see it right now."

Laurie laughed. "It's because both sides of your brain is so small, it can't tell the difference!"

Danny glared at her. "Yeah? Your head is so lopsided; it would make a good ski slope!"

Everybody laughed.

"Hey! You're eating up all the popcorn! Danny shouted at Robert.

"It's so good. I can't stop. You better dig in." Robert started eating faster. Danny rushed over and started eating really fast, too.

"Hey!" Laurie moved over and joined in.

"Well, don't leave me out!" Julie joined the scramble. Pretty soon popcorn was flying and they were fighting for the bowl. A popcorn fight. That was fun.

"Well," Robert looked at this watch. "It's time for me to go. I've got work tomorrow."

"I'll walk you out." Julie said.

"I was hoping you would." Robert smiled at her. He stood up and took her hand to pull her up from the sofa. He turned and said, "Hey you guys, it was so nice meeting you. I had a great time." He stopped in front of Laurie. "You, young lady, make excellent popcorn." He stepped up to Danny and extended his hand. "I give you back your mother now." Danny shook his hand.

"Goodnight." Danny and Laurie spoke at once.

At the door, Julie kissed him lightly. "You probably saved my son's life, you know."

Robert laughed. "He means well. He wants to keep the outsiders where they belong ... on the outside!! It's a tough job, but somebody's GOT to do it." Robert had a gift for smoothing things out. "Will you come with me to my parlor, Madam?" He pulled her close to him in a motion similar to the move Dracula used with his victims.

"I can't. Not tonight."

"Tomorrow, then. Please don't make me wait any longer than that, my Love." He was biting on her neck.

"Maybe. Call me."

"Okay. I'll call you at 6:00 and I'll pick you up at 7:00, how's that?"

Julie hesitated. She loved the way he wanted her. It was very flattering. "I'll be ready."

She opened the door. He kissed her on the way out.

"Goodnight."

"Goodnight." She closed the door. Now she would go and kill Danny!

<u>THE NEXT DAY</u>

Julie could hardly wait. She was so excited. It had been a long time since she felt like this. She wanted to be in his arms and feel his body against her own. She wanted to feel his hot lips on hers as they make mad, passionate, sweet love! "It's my turn." She said softly.

"What time will you be back?" Laurie wanted to know.

"Don't let him kiss you." Danny warned. "I am a man and I know how men are."

"I'll be careful, Danny." Julie was amused. Kids! "You guys don't give your Grandma a hard time. Get in bed on time."

"We will."

The doorbell rang. Danny ran to open the door for Robert. "Come in." Danny extended his hand to Robert. They shook.

"Hi Danny. How are you today?" Robert was a little surprised at this friendly greeting from Danny.

"I'm fine. I'll tell Mom you're here." He ran out.

"Hello." Julie appeared. She walked up to him and brushed his lips lightly with her own.

"And how are you?" Robert asked her.

"I am feeling fantastic!" She really was. "And you?"

"I am wonderful. You are such a beautiful woman."

She looked at him seductively. "You are going to get it!"

"Um... I'm in for it?"

"You are."

"Well then, let's go." He smiled that smile as he reached for her arm to guide her out the door.

Robert opened the car door for her. "I'm starved." He said as he got in the car. "Are you hungry?"

"I sure am."

"What do you want?"

Julie thought for a moment. I want you she thought, but aloud, she said, "I like fish. How about you?"

"Oh, I know the perfect place. They serve the best fish in town! They got good deserts, too. Probably not as good as the one I'm going to have, though." He flashed that smile at her while he stroked her leg under her skirt. Julie was powerless. "By the way, you are really a beautiful lady! You turn me ON! I haven't been able to think about anything else all day." He was pouring it on. Julie loved every minute of it. They pulled up to the restaurant. Robert leaned over and kissed her. She could not hold back. How sweet it was! Julie was thinking about how hard it would be to wait until after dinner. She would have to manage.

Robert's apartment was definitely a bachelor's place. He explained that his "roommate" had taken much of the decorative items. One plant remained and it needed serious attention if it going to be saved.

"I called in the maid," he joked. "I told her to do a special job because I had a special lady coming over and I didn't want her to know I was a pig."

“I'm flattered.”

“Let me have your coat, Madam. Would you like a drink? I have coffee, water, juice, and wine. Which would Madam prefer?”

Julie was amused. “I think I'll have the wine, Sir.”

“On the rocks, or without?”

“Without, please.”

Robert hung the coat in the closet and went into the kitchen. He swung open the refrigerator door and took out the bottle of wine. “Chilled wine. Only the best for Madam!” He smiled at Julie. She got butterflies in her stomach when he smiled at her. Something about those eyes!

“Can I help?” Julie offered.

“Not tonight. No women in the kitchen.”

“That sounds like a chauvinistic remark. Are you a chauvinist?”

“Oh no, are you one of those liberated women?”

“Does it matter?”

“No.”

“Then answer the question.”

“No.”

“No what?”

"No. It wasn't a chauvinistic remark and I am not a chauvinist. Now answer mine." He handed her a glass of wine and sat down next to her on the sofa.

"No."

"No what?"

"No. I'm not a liberated woman, but I do believe that men should share household chores."

"And I believe that women make the best corporate officers."

They laughed. She loved his sense of humor.

They gazed into each other's eyes. Robert moved closer to Julie. He was playing with her hair.

"Do you think it's okay for a woman to initiate and enjoy sex?" She asked as she ran her fingers down the side of his neck.

"You want to rape me? I promise not to tell a soul!"

"You are really something, you know."

"Yeah, I bet Danny told you to tell me that." They both laughed.

"Danny had fun in spite of himself. He tried hard not to like you."

"Really? I would have never thought he didn't like me – I thought he hated me." They laughed some more.

"And I don't think he wanted you to like me either. He tried to show my defects."

"Well, it didn't work. I like you very much." He kissed her passionately. She kissed him feverishly. They were almost on top of each other. She could hardly stand it. She wanted to feel him inside her.

Robert took her empty glass and set it on the table next to his. He took her hand. "Come with me."

His bedroom was very simple and very neat. He pulled her close to him. "You are so beautiful." He kissed her face, her lips... she was melting.

His hand was under her skirt as she stood in front of him as he sat on the bed. He was stroking her. She wanted to scream. "Your skin is so soft." He was unzipping her skirt. It fell to the floor. He stood up and began to undo his own clothes. "You have a lovely body, Julie. I want to see you naked."

"Yes, Sir! Your wish is my command."

"Wow! A woman who obeys? I don't believe it."

"You ARE a chauvinist!"

"Come here. I'll show you what I am." She walked over to him. "I want to please you, Madam. Your wish is MY command." He pulled her down on the bed. "I want you so much." He sucked in his breath. He was kissing her everywhere... his tongue was fast. He moved up to her face and put his tongue in her mouth. She was ready. He entered her very gently. He was good! They couldn't get close enough. Finally, they collapsed. Exhausted, they fell asleep in each other's arms.

"I must be in heaven." Julie thought. "Robert was worth all the waiting. Finally she had won."

The alarm woke them sharply. It was five o'clock.

"I wish I didn't have to work today. I'd love to stay right here in the bed with you." Robert said as he kissed her back.

"It would be nice, but I have to work too. Besides, I should really get home before dawn. You know I have detectives at home who call themselves my kids."

"Come and shower with me. You can wash my back. Remember, I'm the chauvinist, and a woman's duty is to wash her man's back!"

"Yes, Sir!" She followed him into the bathroom. All day she would wonder if he was now "her man".

They pulled up to Julie's house.

"Coffee?" Julie offered.

"No time." He leaned over and kissed her gently. "I'll call you later, okay?"

"Okay. You have a nice day." Julie got out.

"Can't be anything but wonderful, thanks to you, Julie."

She closed the car door. Robert was soon gone. Inside the house, Julie looked at the clock on the kitchen wall. Six thirty. Almost twelve hour of glorious love! She had a little time to herself before the kids wake up. She could daydream while she made coffee. She was floating around. "I wonder if this is cloud nine."

"Good morning, Mother!" Laurie surprised Julie.

"Good morning, Sweetheart. What are you doing up so early?"

"Are you just coming home?" Laurie ignored her mother's question.

"Do you want some coffee?" Julie ignored Laurie's question deliberately.

"No, thank you. I got up early because I was worried about you. Are you just getting home?"

"Yes, Laurie. I am."

"You mean you spent the night with him?"

"You know, Laurie, I have a right to my own personal life. I don't have to answer to you or Danny. You guys don't seem to understand that I am not so old that I don't want to share some of my time with a man. I still need that in my life. Can you understand that?"

"So, is he your boyfriend now?"

"We didn't make any promises to each other, but I intend to see him again." Julie hoped she was getting through.

"Well, did you make him use a condom?"

Julie was so shocked she almost choked on her coffee. "What?"

"You know. With all the diseases going around... you know. Mother... I mean, he could even have AIDS! How do you know what he does or who he does it with? That's what they tell us in my Health class."

Julie's mouth was wide open. She knew Laurie was making sense and yet, it didn't seem quite right that she should be telling Julie, her mother, how to have safe sex.

"It's true, Mom. You have to be careful these days. So did you?"

"Laurie, are you sure you don't want some coffee? It's good for calming people down."

"So, you want me to shut up, huh? Okay. I can take a hint. You really like this guy a lot, huh?"

"Yes. I sure do." Julie's face lit up again.

"Well, to be honest, I'm glad you finally found somebody you like. Since you're my mother, it's hard to see you as a regular person. You know what I mean?" They looked at each other and laughed.

"Yes, Baby. I understand. You know, I don't know where I'd be without you guys. I won't let anybody or anything come between us or take away from what we have, no matter how much I like him."

"Is Robert going to take us out, too?"

"We'll see what happens. Okay?" Julie kissed her daughter on her cheek. "Now, you'd better get ready for school."

"Okay." Laurie started out of the kitchen. She turned around to look at her mother. "You know Danny's not going to be so easy!" They both laughed.

"I love you!" Julie yelled after her.

"Now, let's see what we will have for breakfast." Julie mumbled.

Julie cruised over the next two months. She talked to Robert every day. They spent time together often, mostly at his place. Julie's smile was plastered on her face. Someone mentioned a 'glow'. She decided not to tell anyone. Not yet.

Of course, the kids didn't like the time she spent at his place. Nor did they like the fact that even when she was home, she was a bit removed from them and only thought about and waited for Robert's call. Then she would scurry to get ready for him to come and take her to his place. Julie felt entitled to this love. The time that was set aside for the kids was spent in time arguing against Robert. The kids would have to adjust. They had to know that to love Robert didn't mean that she would stop loving them. The change had some adverse effects, but the good outweighed those for Julie. Would they be happy only when she was alone? Only when there was no one loving Julie? Why should she have to choose one over another?

Then, things began to change. Robert's calls became less frequent. Julie's calls were going to voice mail. When he returned her calls, there was an apology for taking so long. There were apologies for the absences, and for the apparent lack of attention paid to Julie.

One evening, Julie was just getting in from work when the phone rang. It was Robert.

"How are you?" Her voice was soft.

"I'm fine. How are things with you?"

"In heaven, or on earth?" Julie joked.

Robert laughed a little bit. He seemed nervous. "Uh... Julie, there's something I need to tell you. I can't right now, but is it okay if I call you at work tomorrow?"

Julie was puzzled. Why couldn't he talk about it now? "This sounds serious."

"Well," he paused. "I guess it is. I'll get back to you as soon as I can. Okay?"

Did she have a choice? "Okay." She hung up the phone.

Julie wondered what it could be. It wasn't fair for him to leave her dangling in suspense like this. She would call him back and tell him! She picked up the phone, but thought better of it. No, she would wait. After all, if there was something he wanted to share with her, it must mean that he wanted their relationship to get off to a good start. Or, maybe he does have AIDS! Maybe she should have made him use a condom after all. What would she tell the children?" "Damn!" What is going on?

<u>THE NEXT DAY</u>

Julie sat at her desk staring at the phone. He didn't say what time he would call. She looked at the clock. One o'clock. Why did he insist on calling her at work? She would order a sandwich. No, she was going out. She would not spend any more time wondering what Robert had to tell her. Although, she had tried not to jump to conclusions, she felt that he was being so inconsiderate for him to treat her like this. She stood up to leave when the phone rang.

"Hello, this is Julie."

"Hi, Julie. This is Robert."

"I know who you are." She was optimistic.

"How are you?" He asked. She suspected he was feeling her out.

"I'm fine." She wanted to get on with whatever it was that he could only discuss at her job. "What's happening, Robert?"

"Um... listen Julie. I really feel like a heel. There's something I should have told you. I couldn't ... no, I didn't want to lose you. Well, I wanted to keep you as long as I could. I don't want to lose you as a friend either because you are so special to me. I didn't want you to think that I just wanted you to sleep with me and... think it didn't mean anything. At the same time, we are not obligated.."

"Robert, we are not obligated..."

"I know, but something's happened"

Julie held her breath. She knew this was not going to be good. She knew it was not something she wanted to hear.

"Julie, remember I told you that I had a roommate and she had moved out a couple of months before I started seeing you?"

"Yes, I remember." Julie said.

"Well... she moved back in. I know she won't be there for long. That's the way she is. I know it's a bad relationship and it probably won't work again, but... I just can't put her out. At the same time, Julie, I don't want to lose you. I know it's not fair to ask you to wait... but ... will you still be my friend?"

Julie stared at the phone. She was speechless!

"Julie..." Robert was saying.

"I'm here. This is all a little hard to digest right now... I mean, it's so sudden." She stammered.

"I'm sorry."

"Yeah... okay." Julie's mind raced to think of words to say. "I really have to go now. I haven't had my lunch yet." She hung up the phone and stared at it. She was in total shock!

"How dare he... how could he do this?" Julie had a lump in her throat. Tears gathered in her eyes. She fought them back. She would not cry over this... this wimp! She didn't know what to do just yet. Finally, she sighed and threw up her hands. "Well, I guess I can go to lunch now." She gathered herself and left.

At home that evening, it was hard to hide her feelings, especially from Laurie. Julie was sitting on the sofa in the den staring at the TV.

"What's wrong, Mother?" Laurie asked as she sat down next to Julie on the sofa.

"Nothing, Sweetheart." Julie tried to smile as she said it.

"Yes, there is. Do you know who you're talking to? It's me, your daughter. I KNOW when something's wrong with you." Something happened with Robert?"

Julie could not hold back the tears any longer. She told Laurie the story Robert had told her. Laurie moved closer to her mom and put her arms around her.

"He's probably gay!" Laurie said.

Julie looked at Laurie. They both burst out in laughter.

"I'm serious." Laurie insisted.

"Why do you say that?" Julie took some tissue out of her purse. She wiped her eyes and then blew her nose.

"Just look at you. You're beautiful, you're smart. No man in his right mind could resist you. He'd feel lucky to have a woman like you. I think he made up that story to hide the truth. He's either gay, or very stupid!"

Julie admired and appreciated the way Laurie could always make her feel better. She needed that now.

"Thanks, Baby." Julie kissed Laurie. "I wasn't hopelessly in love…" They looked at each other. "But, I did like him a lot. I thought I could screen them pretty good by now. I really thought he was different."

"Yeah, but you can't know some things about a person until you get close." Laurie had a lot of insight to be only fifteen.

"How did you get so smart?" Julie stroked Laurie's hair.

"And you know what else?" Laurie continued.

"What else?" Julie wanted to hear.

"When some things don't work out, it's because there is something better in store for you. There is a man out there who's looking for a lady just like you. You have to be patient. You told me that. Remember?"

"I remember." Julie was grateful for Laurie. Theirs was more than the average mother-daughter relationship. They were friends, too.

"Where's Danny?"

"He's in his room playing."

Julie went to the door and called him, "Danny!"

He came running. "Hi, Mom."

"First, give me my kiss." Julie kissed him. He turned his face so she would kiss his cheek.

"Don't put lipstick on me."

Julie smiled. She really was a fortunate woman. She felt relieved. "Hey! How about let's go to a movie?"

"Will you be my date?" Danny held out his arm for her.

"Laurie and I will both be your dates." Julie said as she motioned for Laurie to take the other arm.

"Me? Never!" Laurie couldn't resist an opportunity to tease Danny. "But, I guess it's the ONLY way you'll ever have a date."

"Only one problem…" Danny ignored Laurie.

"What's that?" Julie asked.

"I don't get paid until Friday." He pulled out his empty pockets. They all laughed.

"It will be my treat." Julie said.

The phone rang.

"I'll get it. You guys get your coats." Julie went to answer the phone.

"Laurie, you have to ride in the trunk." Danny yelled from his room. "I don't want anyone to see you with me."

"Hello." Julie spoke into the receiver.

"Hi." It was Robert.

"Yes?" Julie was surprised.

"Julie, I've got some time now. Can I stop by for a minute? I want to talk to you."

"Talk about what?" Julie asked.

"Well… just some things I want you to know. Plus, I just want to see you."

Julie couldn't believe she was hearing him correctly. What nerve! Who did he think he was, or, more importantly, who did he think she was?

"Robert." Julie spoke as sweetly as she could. "I think we've talked enough already. You can't come over here anymore. As a matter of fact, I would appreciate it very much if you didn't call me again. Now, I have some very important people waiting for me. You'll have to excuse me. Goodbye." She put the phone back on the cradle. All of a sudden, Julie felt great!! She smiled to herself. She looked into the mirror that faced her.

"Hey Girl, you really are OKAY!" Then she shouted, "Hey you guys. Let's go!"

Pain

Once I loved you.

My love saw no goodbyes.

Everything I could muster

From within

I gave

In vain,

For you,

But you,

You wanted more.

Now, I am numb

And you come

With my dream

Of a love

That long ago

Withered and died.

And me?

Now, I want more.

I Love You Still

So many tears I've shed

    For you

I've told myself

    "No more!"

I've tried to call my feelings in

I've tried to lock the door.

But, when the heart

    Is in control,

Feelings go as they will.

And the truth of this matter is

    My friend,

Even now,

    I love you still.

Our Love

I love
  your body
When your sweat
  rolls onto me...
I love
Touching my tongue
  to yours,
And the taste
  so sweet
When we kiss.

I love
  your manliness
And I am breathless
When I surrender
  my womanness to you
For you
  to love.

I love
Touching my toes
    to yours,
And the warmth
Of your body
Sleeping so close,
    still moist
From the making
    of our love.

Invasion of Love

We opened a window
So we could see

Inside you,

Inside me,

But, just when love

Started to invade

Somebody started

To pull down the shade!

LOVE IS AS LOVE IS

"So, what do you think I should do Sara?"

"About what?"

"About Roger."

"Humph! Seems like you take pretty good care of Roger. Seems like you the one needin' help." Sara looked over her eyeglasses at her young friend. "But we all do sometimes!"

"Sara!" It was hard to pin Sara down to a point sometimes. "You s'posed to be my friend. If I can't talk to you, who can I talk to?"

"Well, what difference do it make what anybody say? You ain't go'n quit 'im jus' cause of what somebody say. That's somethin' you gotta make up in yo own mind."

"But, what would you do?"

"Me? Humph... I'd say fuck him! But I told you, you gotta make up yo own mind."

"Didn't you ever love somebody and maybe they didn't act like they love you, but you just know in yo heart they do, an after some time, they start loving you back?"

"Yeah. But by that time I be tired and say fuck him! Long as you lovin them and they know you love 'em, they don't give a shit about you."

"Well, I believe Roger loves me. He's just scared an don't want to show me how he really feels. You know...they think we might dog 'em out if they show they feelings to you."

"So, you be nice and understanding and then he dog you out. So, who is the fool?"

"Sara, you act like you ain't never been in love."

"Love? Oh yeah. That's what they call it when you get stupid for somebody. Yeah, I been in love alright. Everybody gets a turn. I had a few. It took me a long time to learn. Now I don't take no shit offa no nigga. If he likes my ass, he gotta come in the door asking me how he can go about makin me happy. He gotta think about ME... OR, he can keep his ass right on goin; cause now, I am in love with me!"

"But, Sara, Roger DO think about me and he DO try to make me happy sometimes, but he don't want to seem weak… you know, henpecked."

"Well, if he makes you happy, that's all you gotta worry about. An Suga, if it makes you happy, everybody else should be tickled pink!" Sara leaned back in her chair and started to rock as she sang, "Tain't nobody's business, if I do!"

"What about Michael, Sara? Don't you still love him?"

"Yep."

"Well?"

"Well, what?"

"Are you giving up on him?"

"Well, when you doin all the lovin AND all the hurtin, something is really wrong with that! You better give it up or you are committin suicide to you spirit!"

"But how do you know he don't love you? I mean, I know it hurts a lot, but love can win out in the end."

"Yeah, it sho do hurt alright. Here, I thought we was something special. Thought we was really like on, and he said we was just friends. I told him I do not sleep with my friends. Humph! He wasn't no friend of mine. Real friends don't hurt you like that."

"Yeah, but people who love you sometimes do."

"Well, y'all can have that mess. He have to let me know. He have to come to my face an say he want me, even if he don't say "love." See, my idea of love is that two people make each other feel good. If I'm the one who's always got to get the short end, then I got to say fuck him cause ain't nobody gonna treat me like that."

"Yeah, I know. It's enough to make anybody crazy."

"Well... not anybody!" Sara looked over her glasses at Suga. "But, you know, Suga, if love is real, it shouldn't be so hard. I think it's a matter of meeting the right person to share those special feelings with; but you can't make a man be something he ain't. He got to want what you want from the start or you just asking for trouble. Sometimes that means you just gotta wait." She began to sing.. "Some...day...my prince will come..."

"Girl, you are so crazy! There ain't no hope for you, Sara. How could Michael not love yo crazy ass? I know he do. He jus don't want you to know it."

"Well," Sara chuckled. "That make a whole lot of sense to me. Bout as much as everything else they do. I just think they are stupid. They don't know when they got something good. But, you see, we can't make too easy for them. They need to scheme and lie? It's what they call a challenge, but what it is is really fun. They like you better if you act like you don't give a shit about them. You have to play hard-to-get because as long as you act like you don't care, they keep trying. The minute you let 'em know you love them, it's over!"

"But Sara, that's the same reason they don't want us to know when they love us!"

"Yeah, but if a person really love somebody, they can't keep hidin it. It's gotta show SOMETIME! If you start thinking a person love you, but they don't, you letting yo 'self in for a big heartache, and it ain't easy to stop the hurt. You gotta be tough!" Sara

shook her fist. "You gotta say fuck him or he gonna
keep twistin that knife in yo gut. Yo pain starts being
his pleasure, and you be all mixed up inside thinking
it's really love. An he keep on cutting you and you
keep on bleeding til you almost don't have no blood
left. Then, Suga, you won't have to ask nobody. YOU
WILL KNOW EXACTLY WHAT TO DO! That's when
you learn. That's when the foolishness stops? You
will say "Fuck being understanding! Fuck all of the
bullshit! Fuck love! Fuck him! And Fuck his mama!
An then, Suga, YOU WILL BE LOVING YO'SELF!"

THOUGHTS OF YOU, MY LOVE

Since you happened to me,

It seems

You monopolize

All my dreams.

All my thoughts

Are thoughts of you

And it seems that nothing

I've tried to do

Can stop this feeling

That's come over me

And I yearn for you

To come back to me

And all the time

You're gone away

I tell you "I love you"

At least once a day.

I wait and I want

So desperately…

To feel you…

To touch you…

To have you here…

With me!

WHERE LOYALTIES LIE

Stacy Patrick impatiently waited for the school bell to signal the end of another school day. She usually enjoyed school, but was such a beautiful day, she couldn't help but think of all the fun she was gonna have this summer! Next year, she would start high school. She felt all grown up and this summer, she would do some grown-up things!

"I'll be glad when I'm grown up enough that I don't have to be there with him." She caught herself thinking aloud. She looked around to see if anyone had heard her. No one had.

B-r-r-i-n-g! The magic moment had arrived! Stacy became a part of the masses of children running, shoving, and yelling. Some laughter, some threats... "God, I'll be out of this school for babies next year! All this noise... I'll be grown. I'll be fourteen! WOW!!! Stacy started running to meet Donna Sager. They always walked home together. Donna had lived next door to Stacy ever since she could remember. They thought of each other as sisters.

"Donna!" Stacy called out to her. Donna stopped to wait. "Won't you be glad to leave this madness?"

"Yes, JESUS!" Donna threw up her hands. "If I can stay sane that long. I can't believe we only have one more week. I'll be one happy soul!" They both laughed.

"You wanna stop by my house?" Stacy asked.

"No, I can't. I got to wash those dishes and get that house cleaned before Mama gets home. Then I got homework to do. I can't do nothin' til I get through with that."

"Well, I will help you with your homework. We could do it before Monday. This is Friday, remember? Besides, I want you to go to a party with me tonight."

"No you know my mama ain't gonna let me go nowhere. She is SO old-fashioned. She don't let me have no fun. Never!"

"Maybe she'll let you go tonight. Just ask her, okay? Maybe she'll surprise you..."

"Humph..! If she said I could go, she would surprise me."

"Your mother is too strict." Stacy was thoughtful for a second. "Why is she so mean anyway? Are you sure you're not adopted? Have you seen your birth certificate? You should probably check, you know."

"Yeah, it does seem like that sometimes, but I ain't.

"Well, I sure am glad she ain't my mama. I'd run away from home."

"Yeah. Your mama is nice. I wish my mother would visit your more often. Maybe some of your mama's nice would rub off on mine." They laughed.

"What if I ask her?" Stacy volunteered. She really wanted Donna to go. Donna never had any fun. She was always working. She reminded Stacy of Cinderella.

"Then she'll say 'no' for sure. She'll know we planned it."

"Then too, if I got A's on my report card, she might let me go somewhere sometimes. If I wasn't so dumb..."

Stacy stopped walking. She stepped in front of Donna and faced her. "You are not dumb, and don't you let anybody tell you you are. If you keep saying that, you'll be believing that you are."

"Then why can't I get good grades? I study all the time."

"You don't have no fun. Everybody thinks better after they have some fun. There IS such a thing a studying too much!" They had reached Stacy's house.

"As soon as I finish cooking, I'll be over, okay? I'll help you get finished, too." Stacy wanted to assure Donna.

"Stacy, don't count on me going to that party with you." Donna was warning her. "But you can come over."

"Alright. See you later." Stacy was disappointed. Maybe Donna didn't WANT to have fun. She turned up her walkway, "I hope he's not at home. I wish Mama would make him leave. Maybe if she knew…" She opened the door to her house. It stank of alcohol. She hoped her father was asleep. "Oh Bubba, please be here." She said softly as she closed the door.

"Lock it!" The voice startled her. It was her father. Stacy's heart was pounding fiercely. He was very drunk.

"I..is Bubba home, yet?" Stacy tried not to stammer. She was trying to hide the fear that was beating inside her.

"Did you hear me, girl?" He staggered toward her.

"Okay, Daddy." Stacey locked the door. Her brother, Bubba, might be hours getting home. He didn't have to cook or anything. Stacy was all alone.

He staggered back toward his bedroom. Stacy hurried into the kitchen. Maybe if she started cooking, he wouldn't bother her. "Please, God!"

"Stacy!" He was calling her from his bedroom.

Stacy wanted to ignore him, but she didn't want to provoke him. "Yes, Daddy?"

"Come in here."

"Shit!" Stacy dreaded going in there. She walked to his bedroom door.

"Come over here." He said it as he patted the seat next to him on the bed.

"Daddy, I have to cook before Mama gets home."

"Get over her..."

"Daddy..."

"Get over here, now!"

"Yes, Daddy." Stacy was trembling inside. She sat down beside him. The smell made her sick.

"You don't have to be scared, Baby. I ain't gonna hurt you." His hand was on her leg. "But don't you never tell nobody what we do, you hear?" He was touching her vagina through her panties. He started pulling them down. "You hear me, Stacy? You can't tell nobody that your daddy touch you like this. Answer me when I talk to you.

"No, Daddy, I won't tell."

"Here... feel this." He thrust his penis in her hand. Stacy tried to let it go, but he held her hand on it. "Squeeze it, Baby." He moaned. Stacy felt hot tears roll down her face. How she hated him! Yet, she was desperately afraid of him. She had seen him beat her mother and she knew he would beat her, too. He even beat his own mother before she died.

He was kissing her face. She wished she could throw up on him. He pushed her back on the bed. He was pushing her legs apart. Stacy closed her eyes. "Oh, God!"

"Your little pussy is so pretty, Baby." He began to lick her vagina. He raised himself to his knees and opened her legs as wide as he could without just ripping them off, and began to push his penis against her. He was trying to put it in her.

Stacy was crying louder now. The pain was getting real bad. This was nothing new for her. Once she started to bleed. Her mother found some blood in a pair of Stacy's panties and took her to the doctor. She was nine then. The doctor told Mrs. Patrick that Stacy had been trying to put something up in herself. Stacy was hoping her mother would guess. She never did!

He was panting above her now. She knew it was almost over. She tried not to breathe so she didn't have to smell his stinking breath. She wished he would die!

BAM! Somebody's at the door." He was heavy. He could barely roll off of her. Stacy tried to push him. "Ugh!" He was disgusting!

Stacy was trying to stop the tears as she put her panties back on. She went to the bathroom to wash off what she could. The knocking had stopped.

"Thank God for whoever it was. I got to get dinner on before Mama gets here. She's gonna think that I been messin' around." Somebody knocked at the door again. Stacy checked herself in the mirror before she went to open it. It was Donna.

"Bubba's at my house. Said he couldn't get in. I knew you were here. What's the matter?"

Stacy's body shook with a new outburst of tears that refused to be choked back. She couldn't speak.

"Stacy! What on earth is wrong with you?" Donna put her arms around Stacy and hugged her. "Who's here with you?"

"Oh, Donna. He made me do it with him."

"Who?"

"My daddy made me…" She spit out the words. She couldn't stop the tears and she was afraid somebody would hear her. "I can't talk now. I'll have to talk to you later. I have to cook before Mama gets home. She's gonna kill me."

"Are you gonna tell her?" Donna's voice was soft.

"Oh, Donna. I'm so scared! I don't know what he would do to me if I tell anybody. I just don't know what to do."

"Well, I ain't scared of him. I'll tell her for you. You can't just let him keep on doing that to you."

"I'll talk to you about it later, okay?" Stacy was pleading.

Donna hesitated. "Okay. Are you gonna be all right?

"Yes. Please go. I'll come over later."

"STACY!" Bubba ran in the door. "Here comes Mama!"

"Shit!" Now she's gonna want to know why dinner's not on. What am I gonna tell her?" Tears welled up in Stacy's eyes.

"I'll talk to her." Donna was firm.

Mrs. Patrick appeared in the doorway. "Hello." She spoke to Donna and looked curiously at Stacy. "What in the world is wrong with you?"

"Mrs. Patrick. I have to talk to you about something."

"NO!" Stacy stomped her foot.

Mrs. Patrick looked from Stacy to Donna. "I think you better tell me what's going on here."

"Can we go in the bathroom?"

"Yes. Come on. This must be very serious."

Once inside the bathroom, the girls looked at each other. Stacy started crying again.

"Mrs. Patrick," Donna took a deep breath, "Your husband keeps messin' with Stacy."

"What do you mean 'messin with' Stacy?"

"He makes her do it with him."

"Do what with him?" Mrs. Patrick's eyes were on Stacy. Stacy looked down. "Tell me, Stacy. What happened?"

"He made me..." she was crying.

"He made you do what, Honey? If something has happened, Stacy, I need to know. Now, did he hurt you?"

"Yes, Mama. He keeps trying to have sex with me."

"Oh my God!" Mrs. Patrick put her hand over her mouth and stepped back a little. "Why haven't you told me before?"

"Because I been scared. He told me not to tell."

"How many times has this happened?"

"Mama, it happens all the time when I come home from school and nobody is here."

Mrs. Patrick turned to Donna. "Thank you, Donna. Stacy and I will have to talk by ourselves now."

"Okay. I'll see you later, Stacy."

"Yeah, thanks, Donna. I'll see you later." She opened the bathroom door to let Donna out. "I can let myself out."

Mrs. Patrick closed the door again. "You don't ever have to be afraid to tell me anything. Do you understand that, Stacy? I am your mother. I won't let anything happen to you if I know about it, understand?"

"Now, tell me what happened."

"I came home from school and he was drunk. He made me come in the room and he made me take off my panties and he tried to put his thing in me." Stacy was crying. "Remember when you took me to the doctor?"

"Yes."

"Well, that was why the blood was there. I didn't try to push nothing up in me, it was him."

"How long has this been going on?"

"A long time."

Mrs. Patrick looked thoughtful. There was silence.

"I didn't get a chance to start dinner."

"Don't worry about that. Right now, you go rest for a little while. You look like you could use it. I'll get dinner."

Stacy hugged her mother. She was so happy to finally get it out. She was grateful to Donna for helping her. But, what would her father do now? Right now, she was going to take a nap. She sure could use it. Suddenly, she was exhausted.

"STACY!!" Mrs. Patrick's voice was sharp. Stacy sat straight up in the bed. "Come out here."

Stacy got up. "Coming."

It was dark. She must have slept for a long time. She went into the living room where her mother and father were sitting on the sofa. He didn't look angry, but her mother seemed furious.

"Why did you tell your mother all those lies on me, Baby? You know I would NEVER touch you like that. I would never hurt you." He held his head in his hand and seemed to be crying. "Lawd, have mercy..." he shook his head and sucked in a breath. "I been sleep all day. Was it because you didn't get home in time to do your work? You didn't have to lie on me, Baby...."

Stacy's eyes darted to her mother who was watching her intently.

"Mama, I didn't lie. I DIDN'T LIE TO YOU!!" Stacy looked to her mother for the concern she had shown earlier. There was only hatred in her mother's eyes. 'She thinks I'm lying' Stacy was thinking. "Mama, I told you the truth. Please believe me!!" Stacy pleaded.

"Your mother knows me better'n that. She knows I would never do anything like that to you."

A lump welled up in Stacy's throat. She was alone... really alone!

"Mama!" Stacy turned to look at her mother again, but she was met with her mother's fist in her face. It knocked her to the floor.

"I'll teach you, you little bitch! You don't go spreading lies like that about my husband." Mrs. Patrick was on Stacy now, beating her with both fists. Stacy couldn't believe this was happening. What did she do wrong? Why didn't her mother believe her? Her father stood up and pulled her mother by the shoulders.

"Don't kill the girl, Edith. I think she learned her lesson." Over her mother's head, he smiled at Stacy. "She ain't gonna lie no more."

Hurry Darling!

After all the waiting

Now, you've come …

And gone.

My body burns still

From the touch of yours

And the kisses you planted

All over me.

Making me recall

Again and again

The passion so eager,

So delicious,

So sweet!

Hurry Darling,

I want to feel you

Coming again!

New York, New York

"Damn!" Joyce woke up and looked around the room. There were shoes piled up behind the door. "Maybe, I'll clean up today." She had slept on the sofa in her living room. "No use getting in bed by myself!"

There were stacks of newspapers on the table in the dining room. There were papers all over. She reached into a potato chip bag on the cocktail table in front of the sofa. It was empty. "Shit." She sat up. There were clothes lying all over the place – on the chairs, on the floor – everywhere. "I should be ashamed of myself for letting my house get like this." She looked over into the ashtray and picked up a joint. "I'll smoke this, and then, I'll start cleaning up. Humph! Don't nobody have to come in here anyway. This is MY house!"

Joyce puffed and coughed a little. "Goodness, this shit is strong!" She exhaled. "I'm not calling him today." She puffed. "And I might not talk to him if he calls me! All the promises he made me. Humph! He ain't did shit! Well... he did take me to New York that time. We had such a beautiful time." The thought brought a smile to her face. She puffed a little.

"OOOH-WEE!" That man sho' did love my ass then. Course, I only weighed a hundred and fifteen pounds back then. Look at me now." She stood up to look at herself in the mirror on the dining room wall. "How in the world did I get so fat? Well... so what? Ain't nothing I can do about it today anyway!" She puffed. "Oh well, I guess I'll take a shower and put some clothes on." She looked around and sighed heavily. "Then, I'll start cleaning up."

Joyce flicked the switch on the stereo. She liked to listen to music when she got high. She liked to hear it while she showered. She took showers with Ronald often... "At least we used to. He should a married me like he promised. He didn't even tell me when he got his divorce. Six months! He knew all the time that he wasn't gonna marry me. Asshole! That's why he ain't got me now!" The phone rang. Joyce jumped. "That's prob'ly him." She put the remainder of the joint in the ashtray.

"Hello. Oh, hi Dee... uh-huh... a party? Tonight? Lots of guys, huh? ...it sounds nice. Well, I'll have to see. I'll call you later and let you know. You know Ronald and I haven't had much time together lately... he's been so busy. So, I'll have to talk to him first cause he's prob'ly made some plans for us already. Uh-hum... yeah..., well, I'll call you a little later. I should be talking to him soon. Listen, I've got my shower water on. Okay... bye."

Joyce stepped into the shower. Of course, he'd made some plans for them. "I ain't had none in two weeks. He betta take care of that! I have been his woman for ten years! All my girlfriends been married and divorced, and here I am almost forty years old and never been married. Oh well, what difference does it make anyway if you don't stay together? Besides, our relationship is so special. I wouldn't have it any other way. I could never live with Ronald. See him every day? No, no! It just wouldn't work. I'd get sick of him wanting to screw me all the time. PLUS, then I'd have to clean up." She laughed out loud at that. "Forget that shit."

She hummed along with the music as she turned under the hot shower water. It felt so good! She loved hot showers. The phone rang. "That's prob'ly him. He would wait until I was in the shower." She turned again to rinse the soap off and shut off the water. Grabbing her towel from the rack, she ran to get the phone.

        "Hello." The caller had hung up. "He prob'ly can't wait to get his hands on me. I'll call him back because I ain't waitin all day for him.

"7916." It was Ronald's answering service.

"Hi Evelyn, I'd like to speak with Ronald. Would you get him on the line, please, or I can call him at home."

"I'm sorry, Joyce, but he's not in. Would you like to leave a message?"

"Well... tell him to call me back right away. I'll be leaving soon."

"Okay... but that won't be until Monday. That's when he'll be returning. You know... He went to New York."